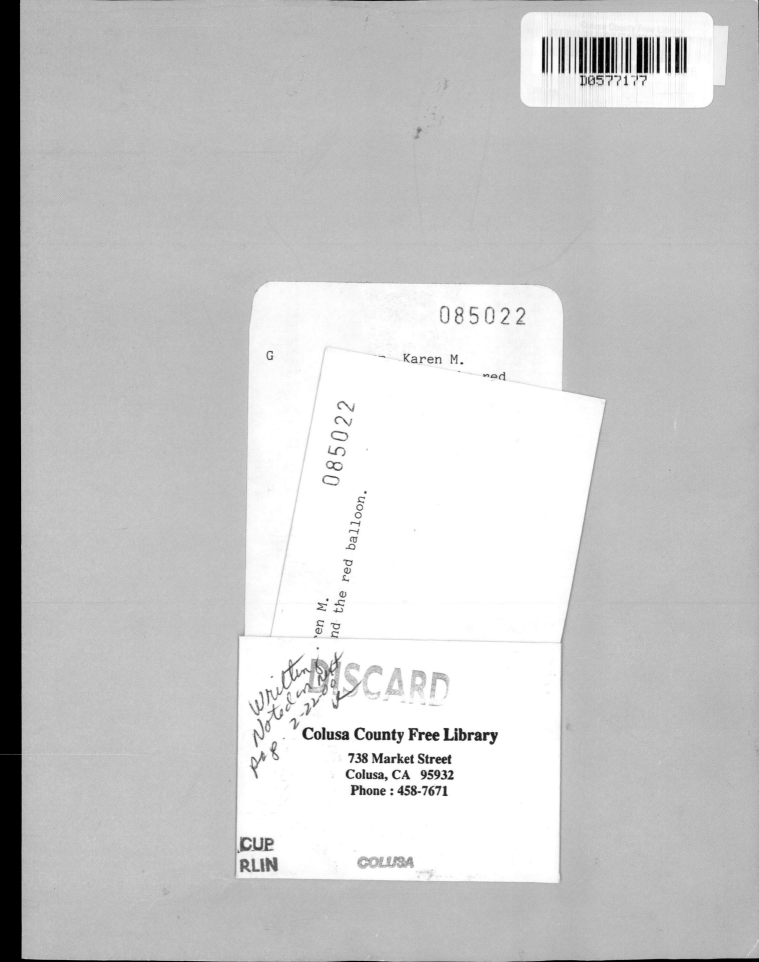

Miss Eva
and the
Red Balloon

4-13-98
DMA

4-13-98
DMA

For my father who gave me the gift of imagination and taught me to dream, and for my mother who gave me the courage K.M.G.

For Felix H.P.

SIMON AND SCHUSTER BOOKS FOR YOUNG READERS
Simon & Schuster Building, Rockefeller Center, 1230 Avenue of the Americas, New York, New York 10020
Text copyright © 1990 by Karen Glennon. Illustrations copyright © 1990 by Hans Poppel. All rights reserved including the right of reproduction in whole or in part in any form. SIMON AND SCHUSTER BOOKS FOR YOUNG READERS is a trademark of Simon & Schuster Inc. Manufactured in Hong Kong
10 9 8 7 6 5 4 3 2 1
Library of Congress Cataloging-in-Publication Data. Glennon, Karen M. Miss Eva and the red balloon.
Summary: Miss Eva, an old-fashioned schoolmarm, leads a routine life until one of her students gives her a magic balloon. [1. Balloons—Fiction. 2. Magic—Fiction. 3. Teachers—Fiction.] I. Poppel, Hans, ill.
II. Title. PZ7.G486Mi 1990 [E]—dc20 89-32515 CIP AC ISBN 0-671-68854-5

Miss Eva
and the
Red Balloon

by Karen M. Glennon

illustrated by Hans Poppel

Simon and Schuster Books for Young Readers

Published by Simon & Schuster Inc., New York

That day Miss Eva wore the same black dress she wore every day.

She left her house at 7:22, just as she did every day.

She passed Spencer's Market and waved to
Mr. Spencer, just as she did every day.

She walked across the street while Mike the policeman held the traffic, just as he did every day.

She walked up the steps of Greenbrier Elementary
School, just as she did every day.

She taught second grade, just as she did every day.

But after Adam Sumner's birthday party,
everything changed!

Adam's father brought colored balloons for
everyone. They were round helium balloons
tied with shiny ribbons.

When Adam went home, he gave Miss Eva
his favorite balloon. It was red with green stars
and moons.

After everyone had gone, Miss Eva got ready to
go home. When she tried to put on her hat, she was
surprised. Her hand wouldn't let go of the ribbon!
Miss Eva had to leave her best hat at school.

Mike the policeman said, "Nice day, Miss Eva,"
just as he always did.

Miss Eva nodded her head, just as she always did.
She hurried across the street, just as she always did.
But today she had the red balloon in her hand.

At Spencer's Market, Joe said, "Nice tomatoes today, Miss Eva."

But Miss Eva had Adam Sumner's red balloon in her hand. She just shook her head and kept walking.

Mike the policeman and Mr. Spencer both noticed
something different about Miss Eva.

Miss Eva's house looked the same as always.

Miss Eva's front room looked just the same as always.

Miss Eva's bedroom looked just the same
as it always did...

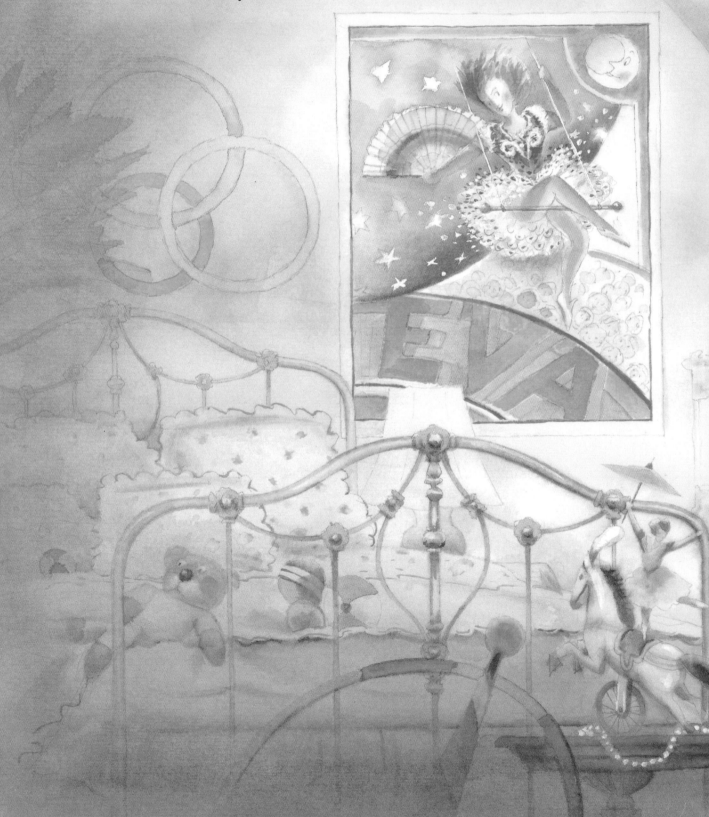

...but today Miss Eva held Adam Sumner's red balloon tight in her hand...

...and something mysterious...

...and magical happened!

The poster in Miss Eva's room began to grow. . .and grow.
The circus came to life!

Soon music began to play, and the lights
from the mirrored ball spun off like stars and swirled
into the night.

The neighbors heard the music and followed the
lights to Miss Eva's window.

The circus performed its magic for Miss Eva's
friends into the early hours of the morning.
Best of all was Miss Eva, who flew through the
night on the wings of her red hair.

The next day Miss Eva didn't wear the same black dress she wore every day.

She passed Spencer's Market and waved to
Mr. Spencer, just as she did every day.

She walked across the street while Mike the policeman held the traffic, just as he did every day.

But today someone new holds Adam Sumner's
red balloon.